Text copyright © 1990 Pat Wynnejones
Illustrations copyright © 1990 Sheila Ratcliffe
This edition copyright © 2001 Lion Publishing

The moral rights of the author and illustrator
have been asserted

Published by
Lion Publishing plc
Sandy Lane West, Oxford, England
www.lion-publishing.co.uk
ISBN 0 7459 4560 0

First edition 1991
This edition 2001
1 3 5 7 9 10 8 6 4 2 0

Acknowledgments

This story is retold from Mrs Gatty's
'Parables from Nature', first published in 1855.

A catalogue record for this book is available
from the British Library

Typeset in 11/12.4 Berkeley Oldstyle
Printed and bound in Singapore

THE TALE OF
GERONIMO
GRUB

Retold by Pat Wynnejones
Illustrations by Sheila Ratcliffe

The village pond was shimmering in the spring sunshine. Bulrushes and forget-me-nots fringed its sides, perfectly reflected in the shining surface.

Below that surface there was a wonderful underwater kingdom, dark and mysterious, where Geronimo the grub and his brothers George and Gerald searched for food and played hide-and-seek, darting in and out of the shadows and shafts of sunlight among the water plants.

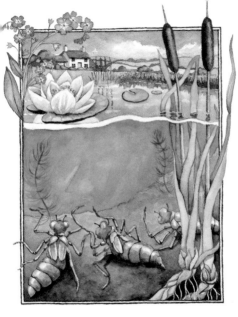

Geronimo was inquisitive. He was curious about the world he lived in, for ever wondering why and asking questions.

'I wonder where the old Frog goes,' Geronimo pondered one day. 'He swims upward to the top of the pond and he disappears from sight – till – Plop! There he is again when we least expect him.'

'Don't be nosy!' his brothers would tease. 'Who cares where the old Frog goes?'

'But do you think he leaves this world?' persisted Geronimo. 'Do you think there can be something – somewhere – beyond?'

'Why don't you ask him yourself?' suggested a young minnow, with a mischievous twinkle in his eye. For the Frog didn't have much patience with questions from young grubs. But at last Geronimo summoned up his courage.

10

11

'Respected Frog, sir,' he began politely, 'if you please, sir, there is something I would like to ask you.'

'I don't please,' replied the Frog, in a rather discouraging tone. 'But ask away, ask away, if you must.'

'Well, sir,' Geronimo said very shyly, 'can you please tell me what there is beyond this world?'

'What world do you mean, little grub?'

'This pond of ours – our world in the pond – I mean, respected Frog, sir.'

'Well, I'll tell you,' replied the Frog scornfully. 'There is dry land. Dry land with beautiful green grass and meadows filled with golden buttercups and sweet white daisies; and there are huge stately trees and blue skies and dreamy white clouds and brilliant sunshine.'

'Wow!' exclaimed Geronimo, but he did not believe it. He could not imagine a world beyond the dark waters of the pond.

'Dry land?' he repeated wonderingly.

'Can you swim about in it?'

'Of course not!' chuckled the Frog. 'Dry land is not water, my little fellow – that is just what it is *not*!' And he blew some bubbles to show his amusement.

'Well,' Geronimo persisted, feeling rather put down. 'What *is* it then?'

'You really are the most inquisitive creature I have ever come across.

Well, dry land is rather like the
sludge at the bottom of this pond,
only it is not wet because there is
no water.'

'What is there, then?'

'Oh, there is air and sunshine and light…'

'What is *air*, respected Frog, sir?'

But this was the last straw as far as the Frog was concerned, for he really was exasperated by all the questions.

'Since you're so eager to find out what lies above, I'll give you a ride up on my back and you can see for yourself,' he offered.

Geronimo was delighted. He climbed onto the Frog's back and up they went – up and up and up!

But the moment they reached the surface – crash! He reeled back into the pond as though he had hit an invisible wall, gasping and panting for breath. He could not live in the air. He belonged to the life of the pond.

He clung to the stem of a water plant, trembling with shock and disappointment, until the Frog swam down and joined him.

'There is nothing beyond
this pond but death,' he wept.
'Nothing but death. Why did
you tell me all those stories about
beautiful colours and flowers and
bright light?'

The Frog regarded him severely.

'I told you those "stories", as you
call them,' he said sternly, 'because
they are true. You know only this
little pond, so you will
not believe
there is
anything
beyond
it.'

He swam away, and Geronimo did not see him until some days later when the Frog returned bearing important news.

'Quick, quick – here!' he called. 'I've just seen something strange – something that should interest you. I saw a grub like you climbing up the stalk of a bulrush until he was *right out* of the water, in the full glare of the sun. Then as I watched there came a rent in his skin and with many struggles there emerged one of those radiant creatures that dazzle the eyes – a glorious dragonfly!'

Geronimo listened in amazement. He could not believe it! 'Was that beautiful creature really once a grub like me?'

As the spring days grew warmer, Geronimo began to feel strange. His eyes became large and brilliant, and some extraordinary force seemed to be urging him upwards, upwards! He began struggling slowly up a bulrush stem towards the surface. His brothers gathered round anxiously, begging him not to go. 'Don't leave us!' they cried.

'I cannot help it,' he gasped. 'I must go.'

'Then promise you will come back and tell us what lies beyond,' Gerald implored.

'Don't forget us,' pleaded George.

'Never!' Geronimo answered firmly. 'I will never forget you. I will return and tell you what I have seen.'

And then he was gone. He had disappeared as completely as the Frog had done.

Gerald and George waited patiently for hours, and then for days, but he never came back.

At last they gave up hope of ever seeing him again.

'He has forgotten us,' said Gerald
bitterly.

But Geronimo had not forgotten
his brothers. No indeed! The Frog
had been right. He had left his
grub body when he left the pond.
He had become a dragonfly, and
risen with glittering wings into the
sunshine. He had not forgotten
his brothers, but he could not
return to them.

He could fly over the green
meadow with its stately trees,
its golden buttercups and sweet
white daisies. He could soar into
the blue skies.

Geronimo knew that one day
he would be reunited with his
brothers. One day they too would
leave the pond. No, he would not
forget them. And one day they
would fly free together.

Text copyright © 1984 Pat Wynnejones
This edition copyright © 2001 Lion Publishing

The moral rights of the author and illustrator
have been asserted

Published by
Lion Publishing plc
Sandy Lane West, Oxford, England
www.lion-publishing.co.uk
ISBN 0 7459 4560 0

First edition 1984
This edition 2001
1 3 5 7 9 10 8 6 4 2 0

Acknowledgments

This story is retold from Mrs Gatty's
'Parables from Nature', first published in 1855.

A catalogue record for this book is available
from the British Library

Typeset in 11/12.4 Berkeley Oldstyle
Printed and bound in Singapore

THE TALE OF
CHARLOTTE
CATERPILLAR

Retold by Pat Wynnejones
Illustrations by Sandra Fernandez

LION
Giftlines

One lovely summer day a fat, green caterpillar was quietly lumbering along a cabbage leaf. Her name was Charlotte. She had not gone far when she came across a white butterfly fluttering feebly beside a little pile of eggs.

'Oh dear, kind caterpillar, do please help me,' gasped the butterfly. 'I feel so ill. I think I shall die. Then what will become of my baby butterflies? Won't you please take care of them for me?'

Before Charlotte had time to think of an answer, she went on.
'You must be very careful what you feed them on when they hatch out.

None of
your coarse
cabbage
leaf. Oh, dear!
I can't think why
I laid them in such a
horrid place! No, you
must give them early dew
and honey from the flowers.
And don't let them fly far
before their wings are really
strong… be kind to them…'
Then the butterfly died, leaving
  Charlotte standing beside the
    eggs feeling very worried
      indeed.

'Fancy asking me to look after baby butterflies!' Charlotte said to herself. 'They'll fly away as soon as they hatch out. They won't bother with me!'

For she had no idea that the eggs would not hatch into butterflies, but into caterpillars like herself.

She did not know that a caterpillar turns into a chrysalis and then into a butterfly. She only knew what it was to be a caterpillar, crawling along. But she had a kind heart, and made up her mind to do her best.

That night she had no sleep, she was so anxious. She spent the whole night walking round the eggs to check that they came to no harm.

In the morning she had an idea.
'I must find someone to help
and advise me,' she decided.
'Two heads are better than one.'
    But whom should she ask?
There was a dog in the garden,
but he was so playful and rough.
He would probably sweep the eggs
away when he wagged his tail.

The cat liked to bask in the
sunshine under the apple tree
and sleep. She was much too
selfish to bother about them.

'I'll ask the lark,' she decided.
'He goes up so high and no one
knows where he goes. He must
be very clever indeed.'

Charlotte could only crawl.
She could never go up high –
so that was her idea of heaven.

13

The lark lived in a cornfield nearby. Charlotte sent him a message, and when he came she told him her problem and asked him how she should feed the little flying creatures once they hatched.

'Perhaps you can ask about it next time you go up high,' she suggested timidly.

The lark only said he might. Charlotte watched anxiously as he went flying up into the bright blue sky, singing as he went. Higher and higher he flew, until she could hardly hear a sound.

She could not see him, because it was difficult for her to look upwards. She could only rear herself up, very carefully. But she soon dropped down again, to walk round and round the eggs, nibbling a bit of cabbage leaf now and then as she went.

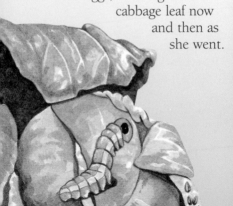

'What
a time
he has been!'
she said to herself.
'I wonder where he is
just now! I would give
all my legs to know!'

Charlotte took another
turn round the eggs.
'He must have gone up
higher than ever this time. I wish
I knew where he goes and what he
hears in that strange blue sky! He
always sings as he goes up and as
he comes down, but he never gives
any secrets away.'

At last the lark's cheerful voice
was heard again. Charlotte almost
jumped for joy as she saw her
friend descend with hushed note
to the cabbage bed.

'News, news, glorious news,
my friend,' sang the lark. 'But
the worst of it is, you will never
believe me!'

'I believe everything I am told,'
said Charlotte hastily.

'Well, then, first of all I will tell
you what these little creatures like
to eat.' And he nodded his beak
towards the eggs. 'What do you
think it is to be? Guess!'

'Dew, and the honey out of flowers, I'm afraid,' sighed Charlotte.

'No such thing, old lady! Something simpler than that – something you can get at quite easily.'

'But I can't get at anything but cabbage leaves,' she replied sadly.

'Well done! You have guessed it,' cried the lark joyfully. 'You are to feed them on cabbage leaves.'

'Never!' said Charlotte indignantly. 'It was their mother's last request that I should do no such thing!'

'Their mother knew nothing about it,' persisted the lark. 'But why ask me, and then not believe what I say? You have no faith or trust.'

'I believe everything I'm told,' replied Charlotte.

'No, you don't,' answered the lark. 'You won't even believe me about the food, and that's only the beginning of what I have to tell you. Why, what do you think those little eggs will turn out to be?'

'Butterflies, of course,' said Charlotte.

'No! Caterpillars!' sang the lark, 'and you'll find it out in time.'

And off he flew.

'I thought the lark was kind and wise,' Charlotte mused as she wandered round the eggs again, 'but he's silly. Maybe he went up too far this time. But I'd still like to know where he goes and what he does,' she added aloud.

The lark heard her as he came down again. 'I'd tell you if you'd believe me,' he sang.

'I believe everything I'm told,' the caterpillar repeated, as solemnly as if it were true.

'Then I'll tell you
something else,'
sang the lark, 'the
best news of all!
You will one day
be a butterfly
yourself!'

'Nonsense!'
exclaimed
Charlotte. 'Don't tease me!
Go away! I won't ask your advice
again!'

'I told you you wouldn't believe
me,' said the lark sadly.

'I believe everything I'm told,'
Charlotte said again.

'At least…' – she hesitated –
'everything sensible. But to
tell me that butterflies' eggs are
caterpillars, and then become
butterflies! You arc too wise to
believe such nonsense, lark!
You know it's impossible.'

'I know no such thing,' retorted
the lark. 'When I hover over the
cornfields or soar up into the
heavens I see so many wonderful
things that I see no reason why there
should not be more. Oh, Charlotte,
it is because you crawl, because you
never get beyond your cabbage leaf,
that you call anything impossible!'

'Rubbish!' shouted Charlotte. 'I know what's possible or impossible, as well as you. Look at my long green body and those endless legs – and then talk to me about having wings and being a butterfly! It's ridiculous!'

'You're ridiculous,' the lark said, 'trying to reason about things you don't understand. Don't you hear how my song swells with joy when I soar up to that mysterious wonder-world above? Can't you take what I hear, as I do, on trust?'

'That is what you call…'

'Faith!' interrupted the lark.

'How can I learn faith?' asked poor Charlotte.

At that moment she felt something at her side. She looked round – eight or ten little green caterpillars were moving about and had already made quite a hole in the cabbage leaf!

They had broken from the butterfly's eggs. Charlotte was filled with astonishment – and then with joy. For since one wonder was true, perhaps the others were too.

'Teach me your lesson, lark!' Charlotte would say when the lark came down to the garden. And the lark would sing about the wonders of the earth below and of the heaven above.

The caterpillar talked for the rest of her life to her friends about the time when she would be a butterfly. But none of them believed her.

Charlotte had
learned the lark's
lesson of
faith, and
when she was
going into her
chrysalis grave,
she said, 'I shall be
a butterfly some day.'

Her friends laughed at her,
but she didn't care.

And when she was a butterfly
and was going to die again, she
said, 'I have known many wonders.
I have faith – I can trust even now
for what shall come next!'